THE
LONG ROAD HOME

Harry Saunders

THE
LONG ROAD HOME

A Journey to Maturity

ISBN: 978-1-4269-5719-2 (sc)
ISBN: 978-1-4269-5720-8 (e)

Trafford rev. 02/02/2011

 www.trafford.com

North America & International
toll-free: 1 888 232 4444 (USA & Canada)
phone: 250 383 6864 ♦ fax: 812 355 4082

THE WRITER'S BIOGRAPHY

The author grew up in New Jersey with his mother, successful father and a twin brother and sister. Harry was a star on the football field during high school years and spent a lot of time on trout streams and camping in the mountains hunting wild game. In his high school senior year he was drafted during World War II for military service in the Navy. Trained as a radio operator, he was sent to the Okinawa Islands and communicated with the fighting troops from an advanced land based radio station during the war with Japan.

After the war, he attended college where he was recalled by the Navy Reserve during the Korean War. This time he was fortunately assigned as a radio operator to the U.S. Navy fleet that toured the Mediterranean on goodwill missions and a show of force. It was during this time that he began to write about his adventures in the military service.

Some of his stories were also published by institutional magazines. He was also paid to write technical manuals under government grant. Later, after marriage and with three children he enjoyed writing unpublished stories for them. It wasn't until after he retired that he commenced writing short stories for publication.

The Long Road Home is his first novel. It could have been the story of his life.

To My Daughters
Susan, Sally, and Cindy

Many ways in this story, Bill is me.

The spirit is mine.

The genes are yours.

To you, I dedicate this book.

…author

Prologue

This is the story of a 16-year-old youth, too young to join the U.S. military during World War II. He runs away from home seeking adventure with the Royal Canadian Air Force who accept enlistments his age.

Hitchhiking his way to Canada to join the R.C.A.F. he experiences exciting adventures. It's a journey that develops his maturity.

Renewed in a new meaning of life, this is his change into manhood.

Chapter One

BEGINNING THE JOURNEY

Bill lowered the backpack out of his upstairs bedroom window on the end of a rope. Dad had gone to work and Mom was mending socks in the bedroom below. She looked up just in time to see the backpack moving past her window and then quickly slipped out the back door and around to the backyard where the backpack had been lowered. She untied the backpack, hid it in the garage, and went back into the house.

In the meantime, Bill was still upstairs composing a note to his parents. He was packed and leaving home. He didn't want them to see him leaving with a pack, but wanted them to know where he was going. "I'm going to Canada," he wrote, "to join the Royal Canadian Air Force and fight those Germans and Japanese."

Afterward he went down the stairs, out the back door and around the house to where he had lowered the backpack.

It wasn't there!

He looked around and decided Mom must have seen it when it passed by her window. He searched around the yard and found his backpack hidden in the garage. Bill shouldered the pack, slipped out the back yard, and was gone.

It was the beginning of his journey. His life in Gainesville, Florida was not as exciting as the books he read. There was a war on. Radio and newsreels at the movies kept him informed of frontline battles. This was the kind of action he had dreamed about.

It was the summer of 1942.

At the age of 16, neither the Army nor Marines would accept him. Too young, he was told, but a rumor had been passed around school that the Royal Canadian Air Force were accepting volunteers his age. He had envied older friends who had already joined up. While on furlough, they had talked about their experience in the military service. Bill decided he was going to Canada where he would be old enough at 16. Now, he, too, was on the way to war.

For Bill, it was a time when the call to arms to defend his country was a call to the biggest adventure of his life. It was a time for excitement and glory.

Early in the morning on a deserted street in Gainesville, Bill hiked with his pack on his back toward the main highway that passed just outside of town. The slim six-foot tall youth with rumpled brown hair and brown eyes looked older than 16. As he walked along the road, he thought about his kind parents and happy home. What would they think? Would they understand what he must do?

When he reached the well-traveled highway, he stood at the edge of the road and thumbed at passing cars for a ride.

A car finally stopped. A man inside the car threw open its door and said, "Hop in."

Bill put his pack onto the back seat and climbed into the front seat.

"How far you going?" the driver asked.

Concerned that the driver might think he was running away from home, Bill answered apprehensively, "I'm going to Canada to join the Royal Canadian Air Force."

He studied the man. He was an ugly-looking character with dark complexion, stained teeth, and a plug of tobacco lumped in one side of his mouth. A greasy cap shielded his eyes, and a dirty long-sleeved shirt, open at the neck from two missing buttons, was partly crammed into stained grey pants.

"Tell you what," the man said, "I could use a guy like you. I got a job for you that won't take long. You can do this and be on your way in no time. It's easy money."

"No thanks," Bill said, shaking his head. Something about the offer did not sound good. He said, "I've got to be going to Canada."

"Yeah, that's too bad," the driver grumbled as he slowed down, pulled off the road and opened the door. "This is as far as you go. I got no room for a young runaway kid that some cop is gonna question me about."

Bill watched him drive away.

He was on an isolated stretch of the road with woods on both sides.

Drivers were not inclined to stop in such a secluded area. Many cars passed. Finally, a car slowed down and pulled off to the side of the road. Bill picked up his pack and ran up to the car. Through an open window, he said, "Can you give me a ride, mister?"

A bald-headed man dressed in a clean white shirt and tie said, "Get in," as he leaned across the seat and opened the door. "I'm going to a revival meeting in White Springs. I'll take you that far."

Once again, Bill put his pack in the back seat and slid in on the front seat.

"I'm a salesman. I sell Bibles," the driver said as he speeded back up on the highway. His idle chatter nearly put Bill to sleep as mile after mile passed. Suddenly, he became fully awake when the driver asked, "Where you going?"

Bill hesitated. It did not go well the last time when he had said Canada.

"I'm going fishing," he said.

"Where are you going fishing?" the driver asked.

Bill didn't know what to say, so he lied, "I'm headed to the Flat Brook River to try my luck."

"Flat Brook?" the salesman asked. "I never heard of that river."

"It's just down the road a piece," Bill said with growing uncertainty as he lied about his destination.

"Well, I'm glad for the company. Let me know when you want to get out."

The miles passed and the salesman droned on about selling Bibles. "You got to know about binders, gold-edged pages, and covers. It makes no difference what's inside or what it's about," the salesman lectured. "Don't believe it when they say you can't tell a book by its cover. It's the cover that sells the book most times."

Bill dozed off for a while, but woke up abruptly when the salesman said, "This is the road where I turn off the highway toward White Springs. You'll stand a better chance catching a ride here on the highway."

The sun was going down. Bill was at a deserted intersection in wooded country. As the salesman drove out of sight, silence closed in around him and it was getting dark.

It's quiet out here. There aren't any cars going by, Bill mused.

An owl hooted from one of the trees next to the highway. Bill was uneasy in the silence. He picked up his pack and started walking.

He had hiked a short distance down the deserted, darkening highway when he came to an opening among tall pine trees growing beside the road. He walked off the side of the road into a wooded glade sheltered by big trees. There he made camp. He was getting hungry and ready to call it quits for the day.

As darkness crept in around him, he got a fire going. He took a small pot and frying pan from his pack and in no time had coffee and hoecake cooking on the fire.

After he had eaten, he felt better and stretched out on his bedroll. The campfire dimly lit up the trees around him. Thoughts of home flooded his memory. What was mom doing right now? What was dad thinking about him? What must he do?

Up through the branches, he studied the dark sky. On the horizon, he saw lights reflecting in the sky. There must be some kind of settlement that way, not far down the road, he thought. After a moment, he decided to hike down the road to see what was there. Maybe he could find something cold to drink.

Leaving his campsite hidden in the glade, he walked down the road toward the lights. He was feeling better without the heavy pack on his back and to himself he was singing, "'Pepsi Cola that's for me, 12 full ounces that's a lot, nickel, nickel, …"

Bill found a combination filling station and store on crossroads about a half mile down the road. Lights were glowing from the station and he could see cars parked randomly around the outside. From inside the store he heard voices.

Bill opened the front door and went into the unfamiliar place.

A group of six or seven men sat on chairs and boxes around an old pot- bellied stove. A foreboding group in drab denim and high top work boots, one or two wore broad-brimmed straw hats, and the rest wore dirty, sweat-stained tractor caps. As the screen door slammed shut behind him, a hush fell over the room and the men turned to look him. Bill spied a cooler at the end of the room. He walked over to the cooler, opened the top, plunged his hands into the icy water, and pulled out a bottle of Pepsi Cola.

"Hot dog," he said to himself. This is better than pulling a big fish out of the lake, he was thinking.

The room had grown quiet, until suddenly the meanest-looking man in the room growled, "Where do you think you're going?"

After a tense moment, he remembered there had been trouble when he said Canada. "I'm on a fishing trip," Bill said.

"Fishing?" the mean looking man yelled. "Don't you know there's a war on? My son is in the army over there fighting Germans, trying to keep from being killed, and you're a draft-dodger, playing around going fishing." He took a menacing step toward Bill and snarled, "For two cents I'd slap the tar out of you."

Bill decided he better get out of there. He put a nickel on the counter for the drink and headed for the door.

The screen door slammed behind him as he ran up the road toward camp. He was out of breath and scared.

Looking behind as he hurried down the road, Bill was alarmed to see the lights of a car pulling out of the station and heading his way. The men from the store, he thought. Quickly, he jumped off the road, into the bushes.

The car drove up the road swiftly and then slowed. A spotlight came on and searched both sides of the road. Bill lay flat on the ground, behind a bush, holding his breath as the car slowly passed. Ahead he watched the car turn around in the road and very slowly drive back. The searchlight continued to work both sides of the road.

Fearfully, Bill watched through the underbrush as the car's lights passed and turned back into the station. He jumped up, and ran to the dark path leading to his camp.   B i l l dropped down on his bedroll, breathing heavily. What were they going to do to him, he gasped.

Chapter Two

HOW FAR IS IT TO CANADA

The eastern sky was just beginning to brighten when Bill woke in his wooded campsite. He had a restless night with nightmares about devils dressed like farmers chasing him through cornfields yelling, "We're gonna gitcha, draft-dodger."

By the time the sun broke through the haze on the horizon, he was packed and ready to go. He was thinking it would be better if he got past the filling station early before any of those harsh-looking men were up-and-around.

No sooner had he set his pack down at the side of the road, when an old Ford pick-up truck appeared out of the mist. Bill waved his thumb and the truck came to a stop beside him. A farmer leaned out the side window and said, "Hop in the back."

As the truck pulled back onto the road, a woman in the front seat beside the driver, slid open the back window and yelled over the noise of the engine, "How far you going?"

Bill leaned back against his pack in the back of the truck and shouted, "I'm going up north to see my aunt who lives in Buffalo."

"We're going to market," she said. "It's about 60 miles up the road. We'll be glad to take you that far."

The truck did not slow down as it drove past the filling station at the crossroads. Bill lay down flat in the back of the truck as they passed. He warily peeked out and saw there was nobody there. Too early in the morning for them, he thought. It's a good thing. I wouldn't want to face up to those guys again. No telling what they would have done to him.

Feeling uneasy, he wondered how far it was to Canada. The old truck labored along the highway, making a steady drone that soon put the adventurer to sleep.

In a little over an hour, the farmer pulled off the road and yelled through the back window, "Okay! This is the market at Macon. You wanna get out here? I'm gonna pick up a load of melons inside to take back."

"I'd be happy to help you load the truck," Bill offered.

"Naw, that ain't necessary. We get them loaded when we pay for 'em."

Bill shouldered his pack, jumped down out of the truck and said, "Thanks for the lift, mister."

As he walked through the market place, a sign tacked up on a telephone pole caught his attention. In large letters across the top of the sign it read:

MAKE MONEY
Pickers needed to harvest peaches. Pay is good Apply today at depot in front of the Market Place.

It didn't take long to find the depot. There was already a line of people applying for the job. Bill got in line. When he reached a desk at the front of the line, an old man dressed in overalls and a straw hat, took his name and explained the job.

"You pick peaches and get paid ten cents a pound for what you pick. Sign yer name on this paper, and be heah tomorrow morning at five o'clock. A bus is gonna take all the pickers to the orchard."

Bill said to himself, he could do that. He signed his name under a long list of names already on the paper.

Wandering by all the trucks at the market place and seeing the loading and unloading of various kinds of fresh produce, made Bill's stomach growl. He recalled he had not eaten all day.

He saw a farmer culling out over-ripe produce from his truck. He had piled up on the ground cucumbers, tomatoes, and a couple of melons that he was preparing to throw away.

Bill was quick to say, "I'll be glad to take those to the dump for you."

The farmer grinned at the hungry boy, traveling with a pack on his back. "Sure, kid," he said. "Help yourself. Here's a head of lettuce and some fried chicken I can add to the pile."

Bill found a remote place among the trees behind the market place, opened up his pack, took out his aluminum plate, and began to chop up some of the cucumbers, tomatoes, and lettuce. The large salad with the fried chicken helped to satisfy the hunger pains.

It was getting dark and he was tired. Hidden in the trees, he opened his pack and took out his sleeping bag. He dug a cavity in the ground, filled it with leaves, and covered it with his sleeping bag. The open end of the waterproof sleeping bag had a long, wide flap that Bill staked up, back over the opening to shield him, like a small lean-to. Wrapped in a blanket, Bill snuggled down comfortable and the sound of crickets put him to sleep..

Early the next morning, Bill packed everything, shouldered his pack and left the campsite. He was the first to show up at the depot. By five o'clock about 75 people had shown up.

They were loaded on to three old city buses being used for transporting farm labor to the groves. In one of them, Bill was able to squeeze his pack out of sight under a seat in the rear of the bus.

It took the buses about an hour to travel over rough country roads to a large grove of peach trees that stretched out over the land as far as Bill could see.

As each worker stepped off the bus, he was handed a numbered badge and told to pin it on the front of his shirt. Given a bushel basket, he was directed to a row of peach trees in the field. Fill the basket, they were told, and bring it to a truck at the end of the field to be inspected, weighed and recorded to their badge number.

"We ain't gonna allow no unripe or rotten peaches," the foreman explained. "Y'er filled basket will be loaded on the truck and you'll get an empty basket. At the end of the day, we'll pay'ya ten cents a pound for what ya picked."

At first, the picking was slow going. Bill was filling baskets with peaches at about the rate of one basket an hour. They took a break at noon, and a tank truck dispensed warm water to thirsty pickers.

Bill ate a peach as he wearily rested and thought of home, wondering what Mom and Dad were doing right now. Mom would be doing the laundry and Dad would be driving to work. They would be proud of him that he could take care of himself. But he was wondering, was he doing the right thing?

A shout, "Get back to work!" interrupted his reverie.

The sun was relentless. Bill mopped the sweat from his brow, trying to keep it out of his eyes. He lost track of the number of baskets he filled with peaches. At first, the picking was slow but after he got the hang of it, he was filling nearly two baskets every hour. Up and down the rows of peach trees and back and forth to the weighing station he trudged. Each step, he thought, brought him closer to Canada.

The day seemed endless. He was relieved to hear the foreman shout, "Stop picking! Get back on the bus."

While they bounced back to the depot on the bus, Bill tried to estimate how much money he made. Gathering his pack from under the seat, he stepped out of the bus at the depot into a line-up of pickers. A cashier was handing out the day's pay. She looked at Bill's badge pinned on his shirt, checked the records, and handed Bill $35.

Only $35! He thought he would make more than that.

Disappointedly counting his money as he walked out of the depot, Bill was attracted to the blinking lights on the front of a White Castle restaurant across the street. It was more than he could resist. He was hungry. Inside he wolfed down a giant hamburger with all the trimmings; French fries, a large root beer, followed by a big slice of apple pie.

As he paid for his meal, he felt that he was counting each peach picked off a tree instead of the money he handed the cashier. What was left, was less than he expected; he would have to pick peaches for another day.

He found the same campsite in the wooded area, unrolled his sleeping bag and fell into it without undressing. He was exhausted.

Early the next morning he awoke as the sun came up over the horizon. It lit up the sky and a few clouds drifting overhead. It was going to be another backbreaking day of picking peaches. He stretched out in his sleeping bag wondering if today he would have enough money. He got up and his arms were stiff and his back ached. It was time to get over to the depot to catch the labor bus going to the orchard.

By tonight, he thought he would have enough in his money-belt. He would have another good supper at the diner in the market plaza and early the next morning set out again for Canada.

Chapter Three

GOLD MINING

After two days of picking peaches, the anxiety to join-up for the adventure he had dreamed about was still an urgent desire. Time was ticking. He had to be in the action before the war was over.

He rolled up his gear in a tight bundle with his sleeping bag, and squeezed it into his backpack. He hiked out of the woods, past the market place, to the highway that was just beginning to get busy. With his pack hidden behind him, Bill waved his thumb in the air. A dozen cars passed before a car pulled off the road just ahead of him and stopped.

Through the open window, the driver said, "I'm going through Atlanta and north to Dahlonega, Georgia. I can take you that far."

Bill looked at a nice man and he decided to tell the truth. "I'm headed north to Canada to join the Royal Canadian Air Force," he said with pride.

"Hop in. I'd like to talk to one of you guys going to fight them Germans. I've given rides to three guys already this week, who were also on their way to join the Army."

"Thanks," Bill said as he swung his pack back in on the back seat and climbed into the front.

It was a long ride on busy highways, into and out of Atlanta, so they had plenty of time to talk about the war. The driver said his name was George. "I'm proud of the way all you young fellas are volunteering to fight. I'd be going too, but our Army enlistment officer at home said I'm too old."

"I'm only 16," Bill said, but I'm old enough in Canada to join the Royal Canadian Air Force. I'm gonna show those Germans and Japanese they can't get away with what they're doing."

They sat in silence for a while as the car was speeding along the smooth highway. George pointed out the window at the mountains that were beginning to loom up on the horizon. "See those mountains over there?" he said. "They say that used to be Indians' ancestral land. There are still a few Cherokee Indians roaming around here, but you never see them. Most of them disappeared when so many white men stampeded through the area prospecting for gold that was found back in those mountains."

"Gold! There was gold here?" Bill said in surprise.

"Yep, Dahlonega was the location for the nation's first real gold rush. They say in less than ten years more than $2 million dollars of gold was shipped out of here."

"When was that?" Bill asked in amazement.

"Well, the gold was discovered in 1828 and a rush started here in 1829. It ended 20 years later when bigger strikes of gold were reported in California in 1848. Eager miners here pulled up stakes and moved to the west coast. However, there are still prospectors roaming around those mountains out there looking for gold. My brother tells the story of a young boy near here who found a yellow rock about the size of a baseball. He took it home and used it as a doorstop in his room. One day, his grandfather was visiting and told him it looked like gold. They took the rock to an assayer who said it was worth $1,000!"

"Wow!" Bill said. "Are they still looking for gold here?" He was thinking, maybe he could get more money for his trip to Canada. Maybe he could find enough gold to buy a bus ticket.

"Yep, there are still a few people prospecting here, but they are not finding as much gold as they once did."

"I turn off here in Dahlonega," George said. "I live just over the mountain. You keep on going north through town until you get to the main highway. It goes all the way up to Canada. Good luck on your trip to join the Canadian army. I hope you stay safe fighting in the war."

"Thanks a lot, mister. I enjoyed meeting you." Bill stepped out of the car, pulled his backpack out of the back seat, and waved goodbye to George.

It was late in the afternoon and the streets were still crowded in Dahlonega. As Bill hiked through the outskirts of town, he came up to a large fenced-in area with a big sign at its entrance:

DAHLONEGA GOLD MINE.
$2 ENTRANCE FEE, INCLUDES
MINING PAN
STAY ALL DAY, PAN FOR GOLD

"Yes! I could use more money!"

Maybe I could make enough, he was thinking, to buy that bus ticket to Canada. He dug $2 out of his money belt around his waist.

An attendant at the gate took his money said, "Good luck," as he handed him a pan, and pointed to a small creek where he saw a number of people panning for gold.

Bill stashed his pack near the entrance where the attendant said it would be safe and shouldered his way between people at the edge of the creek. He knelt down, dug his pan into the bottom of the creek, and brought up a glob of mud. He sloshed water dipped out of the creek through the mud in his pan, Carefully, he washed away the mud a little at a time. It was what everybody else along the creek was doing, checking their pan hoping to see the glitter of gold. What a way to get rich, he thought. Each time after he washed the mud out of his pan, small pieces of gravel remained: none of them looked like gold.

Bill continued panning the mud for an hour, but he was not getting rich yet. Suddenly he saw what looked like a small red stone remaining in the bottom of his pan.

"A ruby," he exclaimed aloud. It was red and small like a bead. It looked just like rubies he had seen pictured on necklaces.

People on both sides of him leaned over to see what he had in his pan.

"It's a red ruby," he yelled again. "Look, I found a ruby!"

A guide, paid to monitor the amateur miners along the creek, shouldered his way through the awed people gathered around Bill and looked at his discovery in the bottom of the pan. The guide reached down, picked up the "red ruby" between his two fingers and squashed it.

"It's a red berry off one of the bushes hanging over the creek," the guide said to the curious people around Bill.

"My ruby," Bill mumbled in disappointment.

It was getting dark and Bill still had not found any gold. He was getting tired but still hopeful of finding gold

At the end of the day, Bill picked up his pack at the gate where he had left it and asked the attendant who was shutting the gate: "Is there a motel near here?"

"Just down the road," the guard said as he pointed the way.

Bill filed out the gate, thinking, "Tomorrow, I'll get rich."

The motel's bed was better than the hard ground he had been sleeping on, but expensive. He took $5 out of his money belt and checked into the motel.

Bill took off his shoes, empted his pockets, and stepped into the shower in his room wearing his clothes. At first, he soaped the clothes he was wearing. Then, after rinsing them off good, he took them off and wrung them out. Each piece was hung separately on clothes hangers and hung up to dry on a line he had strung across the shower. There was just enough room left for him to bathe himself.

He dried off, dressed in the second change of clothing from his pack, and started thinking about eating.

He crossed the road to a restaurant and found a seat in a booth in the corner of the room. He studied the menu and ordered the special for the day: fried catfish with hush puppies, French fries, corn on the cob and sweet tea.

While waiting for his food, Bill glanced around him at the people in the café. Most looked like tourists, except for a man sitting alone at a table. He was well dressed in western clothes. He had the features of an Indian. Tattoos on the back of both hands were very noticeable. I wonder why he's here, Bill was thinking.

A pretty waitress brought Bill his dinner, coyly smiled as she set it down before him and said, "Enjoy." He eyed her cute figure as she walked away from the table.

The catfish was delicious; probably fresh caught, he thought. The bill was $2 and worth it. He even added 25 cents for a tip. His money belt was getting slim. Maybe he'll get rich tomorrow, he thought.

The next morning at eight, there was already a crowd at the gate. Bill had splurged $1 for breakfast and after paying another $2 to get in the mine, he hoped to make a bundle of money panning gold today.

Pan in hand, Bill selected a new spot on the creek bank. He tried scooping larger amounts of mud from the shallow creek. Sloshing the mud with water, he carefully examined the gravel that remained in the pan. Time after time, it was always the same: no gold. However, one miner seemed to be having luck.

Bill recalled seeing him in the restaurant; he was the well-dressed Indian with tattoos on both hands, only now he was dressed like a miner in worn-out clothes and an old straw hat.

Bill watched him when several times he raised his pan and loudly exclaimed, "Gold!"

Hearing this, Bill and several others moved closer, to pan that area in the creek. They watched him lift his pan out of the creek and it was always the same: "Gold!"

Each time he took the gold flakes out of his pan put them in a drawstring bag hanging from his belt and disappear into a thick clump of bushes. Wondering what the Indian was doing, Bill quietly followed him. He was surprised to see the Indian open the bag hanging from his belt and return the gold flakes into his pan. Bill watched the Indian return to the creek and pretend to be mining. Once again, the Indian would raise his pan and yell, "Gold!"

It was a scam, Bill realized. He was not finding gold in the creek. He was pouring the same old gold he brought with him into the pan, and pretending he was making a new find.

"There's no gold here," he said.

He was disgusted with himself for being fooled. He picked up his pack at the gate and headed for the highway.

Chapter Four

LOGGING IN THE SMOKY MOUNTAINS

Leaving the gold mine, Bill walked over to the highway and started hitchhiking. The first car that came along the highway stopped and picked him up. Pulling a camper behind their car, a man, with his wife and young son, were touring through the area. Bill climbed into the back seat with his pack. When Bill told them he had been prospecting in Dahlonega, the man wanted to know about mining for gold. Bill told them of his disappointing experience in the gold field.

"There's no gold there," he said.

"That's odd," the woman said. "The travel book says miners are taking lots of gold out of the Dahlonega gold mines."

"Mam," Bill said, "the only thing Dahlonega is taking out of there is money out of the miners' pockets."

"My name is Sam," the man said. "My wife is Mary and my son is named Larry. He's only 5 years old and enjoys the trip. We're headed for the Great Smoky Mountains National Park. We'll take you that far."

"That sounds good," Bill replied. "I'm going to Canada to join the Royal Canadian Air Force."

Sam liked to talk and for the next 200 miles, he talked about the park. "It opened in 1934 and last year had over one million visitors." Sam went on to explain, "The park has over a half million acres of timberlands, straddling the wilderness ridge that separates North Carolina and Tennessee."

"We have a neighbor who visited the park," Mary said. "He told us about feeding the bears from his car. He said they see a lot of wild animals from the road and the camping is great. We live in Atlanta and we have been looking forward to seeing the park."

"Even with gas rationing, due to the war, we've been saving our 'gas ration stamps' we can make this vacation trip."

It was getting late when they arrived at Bryson City, North Carolina,. near the entrance to the park. Bill said, "Let me out here in the city."

They let him out right in front of Pine Creek Inn motel. Bill checked into one of their single-room units and paid $7 for the night. The bulge in his money belt around his waist was almost gone.

A notice caught his attention:

```
+-------------------------------------+
|              WANTED                 |
|   STRONG MEN TO WORK IN             |
|   THE FOREST. PAY IS GOOD           |
|       EXPERIENCE NOT                |
|          NECESSARY                  |
|    SEE DESK CLERK FOR               |
|           DETAILS                   |
+-------------------------------------+
```

Bill walked back to the front desk and inquired about the notice. The clerk looked at him for a minute, as if he was sizing him up. Then the clerk explained, "The Smokies Lumber Company is looking for lumberjacks to work in the forest near the park chopping down trees and hauling them to the lumber yard. Pay is $50 a week with food and a bunk. If you're interested, and think you can handle the job," he added with a grin, "call this number."

The clerk handed him a slip of paper with the lumber company's telephone number and pointed to the telephone across the lobby. As Bill walked across the room he was thinking, he was running out of money and needed more to get to Canada. If he can handle picking peaches ten hours a day, he was sure he could be a lumberjack.

A rough sounding voice on the telephone took his name and told him their office was in Maggie Valley near the village of Cove Creek. "Be here at 7 o'clock tomorrow morning," he said and hung up.

The desk clerk told Bill, "The lumber camp's office is about eight miles down the road to Maggie Valley. One of the lumber-truck drivers is staying here tonight. You might ask him for a ride. He's in room 14."

A radio was playing loud inside when Bill knocked on the door of room 14. A husky man in an undershirt answered the door. His tattooed arms were so big they looked like logs.

Puzzled, the man looked at Bill as he explained he was applying for a job at Smokies Lumber Company at 7 o'clock tomorrow morning. "If you could ..." Bill began.

The big man interrupted Bill before he finished what he was saying and said, "Sure, I'll be glad to give you a lift. I am leaving at six in the morning. Meet me at my truck out front in the morning."

Bill got a candy bar and Coke at a dispensing machine just outside the lobby. The lump in his money belt around his waist was nearly gone. Bill needed this job. He walked inside his room, picked up the room telephone, and requested a "wake up" call with the motel operator for 5 a.m. and went to bed early.

It seemed like he had just gone to sleep when his telephone rang. The motel operator said, "Good morning. It's 5 o'clock."

A quick shower, and after Bill dressed he grabbed his pack and checked out of his room. He found the driver in the parking area checking his truck and trailer.

"You're early," he said to Bill. "I'm glad you're here so soon. I was hoping to get an early start this morning. I may be able to get them to load me by eight at the lumber company. Hop in and we'll be on the way."

Smokies Lumber Company in Maggie Valley was only a few miles down the road from the motel, The driver was so busy checking his gauges on the instrument panel he didn't get a chance to talk.

The Smokies Lumber Company spread out along the road in a number of buildings. A sign indicated the location of an office in one of the buildings. Logs in neat stacks behind the buildings extended back as far as Bill could see.

Inside the office, file cabinets lined up against the back wall, and a bench, two chairs, and a desk, filled up the rest of the space. On the desk, there was a rough slab of wood with the name DOUG carved in it. Behind the desk sat a husky, weathered looking middle-aged man with his sleeves rolled up. He looked up at Bill.

"I uhhh, I'm looking for a job," Bill stammered

The man scrutinized Bill and said. "You look kinda young."

Gathering strength, Bill straightened up and forcefully replied, "I've had experience chopping wood. I can follow directions. I want the job."

The man studied Bill for a moment and then said, "I need help. I'll give you a try. Our employment office is further back in the yard. They'll sign you up and get you some decent shoes, working clothes, and assign you a bunk. My name is Doug Johnson. As soon as you get settled, come back here and we'll start you to work."

Bill found another building among the stacks of timbers where the employment office was located. Nearby, a larger building looked like a dining hall and bunkhouse. He could see smoke coming out of the chimney on one of the buildings, and smelled bread baking. Bill suspected this was were the kitchen was located.

A bell on the front door of the employment office jingled as Bill opened it and walked inside. A slim man dressed in dungarees with a stained apron wrapped around his waist, met him.

"Howdy," the man said. "My name is Jake. Doug just called me from the drive-in shack and said you would be working here. I'm the clerk, cook, and all around mother, nurse and minister," Jake said with a laugh. "Come with me and we'll get you signed up and give you some working clothes."

Later, wearing his new high top shoes and heavy-duty work clothes, Bill stowed his old clothing and pack in a locker beside his bunk. He was ready to go to work and headed back up front to the drive-in shack. Bill was anxious to see what Doug had for him.

When Bill walked into the shack, Doug was talking to three men. "Oh, there you are,"

Doug said to Bill. "This is your work crew. They are going back out to the woods and will show you the ropes. They are my best crew. They'll make a good lumberjack out of you."

"I'm Shawn, your foreman," one of the men said as he stepped forward. "Follow me, we're ready to go." As he led Bill out the door, he introduced him to Carl and Roy.. "They will be working with you. Carl is an old timer, who has been around here nearly as long as I have. Like you, Roy is a newcomer, just getting started. Listen to Carl and you'll get along just fine."

"Okay, I'm ready," Bill nervously said. "Just show me the way and I'll keep up."

Shawn led the way to a big, yellow van that looked like a tank. He cranked it up as Carl and Roy hopped on a running board. Carl beckoned Bill to hop on beside him.

"Hang on," Carl said, "it's a rough ride out to the slope."

Shawn drove the heavy van through the woods.

Bill was surprised at how fast the van was going. There was no road and more than once he thought the rough ride was going to throw him off the running board.

When they arrived at a thick stand of pine trees, Shawn got out and went to the back of the van. From a storage compartment, he pulled out a long two-man crosscut saw along with three axes and a ten- gallon thermos of water.

"The surveyors have blazed marks on the trees to be cut down," Shawn said to Carl, Roy and Bill. "Cut down those trees so they fall down hill. Carl, you know how that's done. I'll be back around noon, with some grub, to see how you're doing." With that said, Shawn drove off through the woods to supervise other crews.

Bill stood there looking at the pile of tools. "What do I do, now," he said?

Carl walked up to the thermos, drank some cold water and as he wiped his mouth said, "I've done this before. I'll tell you what to do."

Taking time with his drink, Carl screwed the cap back on the water bottle and said to Roy and Bill, "Take the long two-man saw over to that tree lowest on the slope that's marked with a slash. I'll show you where to start sawing so the tree falls down hill."

With Roy and Bill standing on each side of the tree, holding the ends of the saw, Carl said, "Just take it easy. Each of you pulls the saw back and forth across the trunk. Don't push. I will notch the tree with an axe on the spot opposite where you are sawing. Get back out of the way when the tree starts to fall. It might kick back and you don't want to get hit by it."

Bill looked at Roy and said, "I'm ready to run now."

Impatiently, Carl said, "Don't worry about it. If you're not paying attention you won't have time to run. We won't have to untangle your remains from the tree, if you'll move up hill with me when the tree starts to fall.

They cut pine trees to about 24 inches in diameter. Larger trees that measured as much as 48 inches and pointed 150 feet up into the sky were left standing. Bill and Roy, holding each end of the buck saw, climbed up the slope around back of a smaller tree marked with a slash and stretched the saw across its base. Then each started pulling and pushing and right away jammed the saw.

"No," Carl said. "Each of you should only pull on the saw. You pull it back and forth. If either one of you pushes you jam the saw."

It took them an hour to saw half way through the trunk of the tree. Bill was sweating profusely, and cussed every time they both pushed at the same time and jammed the saw. Finally, they got into the rhythm with both alternately pulling and started making some headway. Carl notched the other side with an axe and soon the tree started to sway.

"Get back," Carl shouted as the tree began cracking at the base like a giant groaning its last breath. Bill and Roy jumped back and up hill as the tree came crashing down on to the forest floor.

"Okay," Carl shouted in glee. "Let's see how many more we can topple before Shawn brings us our lunch."

"Come on," Bill shouted to Roy. "That wasn't so hard. We can cut down more."

Carl said, "Make sure you make your cut on the uphill side of the tree, opposite and just above my notch on the other side. I don't want to have to dig you out from under the fallen tree."

Bill and Roy looked at each other. Bill said, "I'm not going to wait for Carl to tell me which direction to run. I'm just going to run up hill where he is."

When Shawn arrived with their lunches, they had three more trees lying on the ground.

"Nice going," Shawn said as he got out of the big panel truck, and inspected the area. "Bill and Roy, you're learning fast. After you've finished your lunch, start cutting off the branches and top the four trees you cut down, Carl will show you how."

" The pickup-dragger will be here by the time you finish. Help the dragger down to the road with your trees. Pick up a ride with the bus after the dragger takes you and your timbers to the mill." After those instructions, Shawn drove off. He supervised six other work-teams. He was a busy supervisor.

Lunch was two sandwiches, each with a thick slice of baloney between slices of rye bread slathered with mayonnaise, mustard and a dill pickle. A cold can of tea, a pack of potato chips, and a chocolate bar came with the two sandwiches. The three men sat down in a shady spot and ate.

"Do you do this every day?" Bill asked Carl as they were eating.

"Every day, as long as I've been here," he replied.

Bill looked puzzled and said, "Is there no end to the trees here?"

Carl said, "I heard there's over 200,000 acres of wilderness owned by the park, which the government is trying to take over. In the mean time, the lumber company has a grant to thin out trees. There are more trees here than we can cut down in our life time,"

When the big yellow dragger arrived, Carl, Roy and Bill had just finished cutting off the branches and topping four trees now lying on the ground. One by one, the heavy machine lifted the big end of the tree and dragged it down 500 yards to the forest road where the fallen trees were maneuvered onto a trailer by the dragger's lifts.

As soon as the truck and trailer were loaded, it departed to the mill about 15 miles away. Carl, Roy and Bill climbed onto the truck and went to the mill. Tools were left at the site for Shawn to pickup later in his panel truck.

It was getting late and the three new lumberjacks were ready to quit for the day. Bill was feeling worn out. He hadn't done so much work in a long time. He lifted his arms in the air and felt the strain in his back. He was going to be well exercised when he arrived at his destination in Canada.

By this time, there were about 25 other lumberjacks at the mill waiting for a ride back to camp. Soon, one of the labor buses arrived and, pushing and shoving, they all managed to squeeze aboard.

When the lumberjacks got back to the bunkhouse, they wasted no time stripping off their dirty, sweaty clothes, and taking a shower. A boisterous group, laughing and joking, they were feeling better after a cold shower.

Two cooks had prepared dinner. Tonight, they had cooked country-fried steak, mashed potatoes covered with gravy, greens seasoned with fatback, a vegetable mix of peas and carrots, and freshly baked corn bread. With it, were the makings for a salad.

Bill filed past a steam counter and had hot food ladled onto his plate. In a separate bowl, from a salad bar he selected lettuce, a choice of tomatoes, cucumbers, pickles, black olives, sliced onion, celery, sliced mushrooms, pickled beets, cottage cheese, sliced green pepper and Blue Cheese Dressing.

"That's better than I've been cooking, while traveling on the road," Bill said to Roy, who was standing in line in front of him.

On a tray, Bill took his food to a table, covered with clean, decorated tablecloths. Each table was set with napkins, eating utensils and usually a vase of wild flowers. The hungry lumberjacks ate their food and talked boisterously about their day.

Bill had never eaten so well. Better than the finest hotel, he was thinking.

The next day dawned with clear blue skies. They were all in the dining room eating breakfast when Shawn came up to Bill and said,

"Doug Johnson wants to see you in the office when you're finished eating."

"The camp manager wants to see me," Bill was wondering as he walked over to the office building. "What did I do?"

Sitting behind his desk, Mr. Johnson greeted Bill as he came in the door, waved him to a chair and immediately started explaining why he wanted to see him.

"The company's Safety and Employment Board called me about the Social Security number listed on your employment application. They informed me Federal Records show that you are only 16 years old. You are less than the minimum age allowed by our Workman's Compensation Insurance. Our insurance company will not cover you. Your work has been satisfactory but I regret that we are going to have to terminate your employment."

"He was being fired!" Bill slumped down in his chair and did not know what to say.

Mr. Johnson went on to say, "We'll give you a day's pay and take you back to Bryson City where you signed up with us. I'll have someone take you back there this morning."

Dejected, Bill returned to the bunkhouse to pack his things. Some one asked, "What did he say?"

"Aw, he said I was too young," Bill sadly replied.

He said goodbye to all his new friends, who were just now getting ready to get on the labor bus to the wilderness area. Bill walked back by the office and they gave him his pay.

Bill asked the driver of the company car to take him to the highway. He looked back, sadly nodded farewell as he was driven out the gates of Smokies Lumber Company. Worried if he had enough money, but looking ahead, he was going to Canada. There, he'll be old enough. They are accepting 16 year olds.

Chapter Five

SHARK !

There weren't too many cars on the road in the morning. It took a while before a blue, late model Ford pulled over and the driver beckoned Bill inside.

The driver was wearing military fatigues.

"Howdy," he said as he shifted up to speed on the highway, "where you going?"

"I'm going to join up and fight those Germans and Japanese."

"I see a lot of you guys rushing out to fight this war," the driver said. "I'm attached to the marine barracks at Little River." He looked at Bill and said, "My name is Jason. I am in the military police. I have duty today guarding the gates at the base. I'll take you as far as I go."

"That'll be great. My name is Bill."

"OK, Bill, just settle back in the seat and enjoy your freedom while you can," Jason said with a grin.

The miles passed and Bill leaned back against the seat and went to sleep.

It was a long ride on the main highway going north.

Bill was stirring in his seat. Waking up, he looked out the window and saw the bay. Surprised, he sat bolt upright in his seat. This did not look like his map said was the way to Canada. Astonished, he said, "Where are we?"

"We're near Norfolk. It's only a few more miles to the military base where you can enlist."

"But I can't join up in the United States," Bill shouted. "I'm too young! I am headed to Canada where 16-year-olds can enlist."

"You didn't say you were going to Canada. You only told me you were going to a military base to sign up," Jason said.

"Let me out," Bill shouted.

Jason brought the car to a stop at a busy intersection.

Bill jumped out and grabbed his pack off the back seat, yelling, "I'm going to Canada!"

He ran across a busy intersection and threw up his thumb to the first car going north. The car suddenly stopped, holding up traffic.

The driver threw open his door and shouted, "Get in, quick! The ferry is leaving."

Bill had no idea where he was and was on a ferry before he knew there was one. "I didn't know you were in line to drive onto a ferry," he shouted once again. "I'm going to Canada to join-up."

"This is the only route going north from here," the driver said. "The ferry takes us to Cape Charles, Maryland, on the Wachapreague peninsula. The road on it is old, but it's the only way going north from where you can go to Canada."

Bill was dumbfounded. He did not realize the car he had jumped into was at a busy entrance to a ferry. He had twelve miles on the ferry to cool off. At least, he kept telling himself, it was going in the right direction.

"I'm only going a short distance to my turn off to Eastville," the driver said when the ferry docked at Cape Charles. "The main road runs along the beach but there aren't many cars this time of day. You will have better luck catching a ride in the morning. Bathers, campers, and fishermen run up and down this road early. You may want to think about camping on the beach. Other than maybe a turtle, you won't be bothered by anyone," he said with a smile.

When the driver reached his turnoff to Eastville, he pulled off to the side of the road and opened the door .

Bill thanked him and waved as he drove away. He looked around. No other cars were visible in either direction. Except for the surf breaking on the beach, it was quiet. It was a moment when he felt all alone. Home was a long way, away. Was he doing the right thing?

The road led north, straight up the peninsula through the dunes with the Chesapeake Bay on one side and the Atlantic Ocean on the other side. He picked up his backpack and started walking on the deserted road until he saw an opening through the dunes on the ocean side.

Bill turned off the road and slogged his way through the sand between the dunes. He found a place to make camp a short distance from where the waves of the Atlantic Ocean splashed up on the beach. Looking one way and then the other, the beach line extended out of sight in both directions. Out on the ocean, no boats were in sight. This was a remote, isolated area.

He was hot and sweaty. It didn't take long to decide this was the place for a swim. A quick glance in all directions assured him he was alone. He took off his clothes, ran down to the shoreline and jumped in..

As Bill swam into deeper water, he became aware that small fish were leaping out of the water all around him. The water, he saw, was shadowed by a large school of fish, rapidly swimming along the shoreline. He had entered the water right in the middle of a large school of baitfish. Why were all these fish being herded up to the beach? Some were even leaping out of the water onto the beach.

Standing in waist-deep water Bill realized, something must be chasing the school into the shallow water. That something, it dawned on him, was a larger fish and he was right in the middle of its frenzied feeding. As he swam back toward shore, among the leaping fish, he looked back, and saw a large fin cut through the water on the surface as the baitfish scattered. It was a shark!

Frantically, Bill splashed his way up onto the beach!

Fish that had jumped up on the beach wiggled back into deeper water. Then it occurred to Bill, those could be his dinner. He started gathering the fish that landed on the beach before they made their way back into the ocean.

Walking back into the dunes to his campsite, he dressed and gathered driftwood deposited by high tides over the years. While a campfire was catching on to the dry wood he had placed on it, he cleaned the fish. Around the edge of the dunes, he chopped down some tall green saplings and erected them in the sand to hang over the campfire. With some wire leader from his fishing tackle, he fastened four of his small fish to one of the saplings. Hanging by the tail over the hot coals of the campfire, it took about 30 minutes for the fish to char. Using his knife, Bill peeled off the skin of the cooked fish and cut off chunks_of fish from the back bone. It was a delicacy, he decided, as good as anything from a restaurant.

After a while, he unrolled his sleeping bag on the sand and nestled down in it.

He laid back, looking at the bright stars in the dark sky above, wondering how much further it was to Canada. He was worried about getting low on money. This trip to join-up was taking longer than he expected.

Chapter Six

THE GERMAN SUBMARINE

Mesmerized by the sounds of the ocean, he went to sleep --- until the quiet pulsating of an engine awakened him. He looked out over the ocean. By the light of the full moon, he saw beyond the surf what looked like a long boat, its hull low in the water.

Suddenly he realized, it was a submarine!

What was a submarine doing here? In the dim light, Bill could see a swastika painted on the side of the conning tower. It was a German sub, he said to himself in amazement. What could he do?

Suddenly the war had come to Bill. He had no gun and not even a rock on the sandy beach to throw. All he could do was sit there and watch.

The sub was close to the beach and near enough in the moon light for Bill to see shadows of three men on deck as they climbed into a small inflatable boat alongside the sub. It took them just minutes to paddle away from the hull and come onto the beach. He saw one man drag the boat out of sight behind the dunes.

In the dim light Bill saw two of the men, supporting a third, as they made their way down the beach. Wondering what was happening Bill followed, ducking behind them through the dunes. After a while, he saw them cross over the road toward a house that had a porch light glowing through the night. Bill sneaked in very close to the house and saw the two men in the shadows lay the man they were supporting on the porch. One of them pounded on the door a number of times, and then both quickly departed back in the direction they had come.

From the dunes, were he was hidden, Bill saw a man inside the house open the door and lean over the body lying on the porch. The man looked around the front of the house, and then Bill heard groans as the body was dragged inside.

In less than an hour, from his hiding place in the dunes where his curiosity held him, Bill saw a patrol car with its light flashing drive up to the front of the house. Then, he saw the injured man, holding his side and crying out in pain, as he was supported into the patrol car, and it sped away down the road.

Bill returned to his camp in the dunes. He had a restless night wondering what he should do. When the sun began to light up the horizon, he saw, as he sat up in his sleeping bag, the submarine was gone. He must go back to the house, he decided, and tell them what he knew.

As Bill was walking up to the house, a white car arrived with an emergency red light flashing on the roof. On the side door of the car, letters and an insignia identified it as the sheriff.

Excitedly, Bill rushed up to the sheriff in his car and said, "I have something to tell you about what I saw happen here last night."

The sheriff raised a quizzical eyebrow. Looking at Bill, he said, "What?"

Standing next to the car, Bill said, "Last night, I was camped on the beach and I saw a submarine come in close to the beach. Three men came ashore. One of them was injured and he was carried to the house. Two of the men hurriedly left leaving the injured man. This morning the submarine was gone."

Still sitting in the car, the sheriff picked up the microphone on his radio and called his office.

There was going to be an investigation Bill was thinking as he slipped away unseen through the dunes while the sheriff was talking on his radio. They would want to know why he was there. Bill did not want to get involved with questions about where he was going. The sheriff would be asking how old he was and where did he live. He was going to Canada to join-up and didn't want to be delayed any longer. He picked up his pack and headed for the road.

Back on the road with his pack on his back there was a lot of traffic going south. Bill guessed it was going to the house. However, there was one car going north, in the other direction. Bill threw up his thumb and got a ride.

The driver was obviously very excited. "I've just been at a house back there," he told Bill. "We got a tip from the sheriff's office at the newspaper where I work, that a German sailor had washed up on the beach. Reporters from all over the place were all shouting questions and talking at the same time. It was very confusing."

"What did the sheriff say?" Bill asked. He was wondering what happened inside the house.

"I don't know," the driver said. "Everybody was so excited, yelling at the same time. I couldn't understand the sheriff. I don't think he knew what to say. Finally, the sheriff got so mad at all their questions, he ordered everybody out of the house. It was a real mess. I left."

Bill said, "How would you like to know what really happened back there?"

The reporter looked at Bill.

"I'm going to give you a scoop," Bill said. To himself, he was thinking, it would be good to tell the reporter what happened. He didn't want any further delays explaining everything again to the sheriff. "Just say you got the story from some one camping on the beach."

When they arrived in Salisbury, the reporter drove to his office. Bill did not wait to say goodbye. He watched the reporter rush inside and he left.

Chapter Seven

THE HEAD BOAT

Bill walked down Main Street in Salisbury past a roadside diner. He could not resist going in. A cup of coffee and a doughnut would be nice, he thought. He had enough money for that.

Inside the diner, he sat at the counter next to a man talking to the cook about fishing. Dressed like a boat captain, he heard the man say, "I've got a charter tomorrow with a group of men from the fishing club, and one of my deck hands is home sick.

On the other side of the counter, Bill heard the cook, who was leaning on the counter in his kitchen apron, say to the captain, "You've got a good deck hand with Stan. Won't he be able to handle the fishermen?"

"Stan is a good rigger," the captain said, "but there's going to be ten anglers .That will be more than Stan can handle. I need to find another deck hand by tomorrow morning."

"Pardon me," Bill interrupted. "I'm looking for a job, and I could be your deck hand. I know about boats and fishing." To himself he thought, well, I've read about it.

The man turned to look at Bill, "Do you have experience as a deck hand on a party boat?"

I want this job, Bill was thinking and he replied, "I can do everything on a boat."

"Well, you look kinda young, but I'm desperate. One of my regular deck hands is out sick and I need someone in the morning. If you can rig lines for a bunch of eager anglers, keep them untangled, net their catch, and clean their fish, we pay $10 a day. If you're helpful to these fishermen, you might also receive tips."

"I can do that," Bill said.

"Okay, I'm Captain Willis. My boat is the *Fish Chaser*. It's in a slip at the Ocean City docks. I have ten fishermen signed up for tomorrow morning. You will have half of them on the port side to take care of. Be there at 6!"

"Thank you," Bill said. Then he asked, "Do you know of a motel around here close to the docks?"

"Son," Captain Willis replied, "there's a motel just down the road from the docks. Many of my customers have stayed there and they tell me it's a nice place. I'm on my way to the boat now. I'll take you down there."

The motel was a long, single-story building that stretches out among the willows near to the beach. Bill checked into the motel feeling good about getting a job. He was down to the last of his money, just enough to pay for the room. Captain Willis seemed like a nice person; maybe he could work for him a few days and make enough money to continue his trip to Canada.

Bill checked into the motel and left a wake-up call at the desk for five o'clock.

Five o'clock in the morning came around too fast for Bill. He barely had time to shower, grab a cup of coffee at the motel, then walk down to the dock where the *Fish Chaser* was tied up.

Captain Willis was already on board, checking the motor, fuel, bait, and food for the run out to the fishing grounds. Bill walked down the dock toward the boat and met him at the stern of a 42-foot fishing boat.

With a frown, Willis said, "You going fishing wearing those north woods clothes? Take off those heavy boots before you come aboard, and come down in the boat cabin with me. I have a cotton shirt you can wear. but you'll have to get rid off those boots and go barefoot. Those wilderness pants you are wearing will have to do. Roll 'em up at the cuffs and you'll get by."

Bill was introduced to Stan by Captain Willis. "Stan is the deck hand who will be taking care of the fishermen on the starboard side of the boat while you are taking care of fishermen on the port side. You'll have to step lively to keep your fishermen's lines baited and in the water."

Stan said, "Howdy." Dressed in jeans and a cool cotton shirt, unbuttoned half way down the front showing, bleached hair on a well, tanned chest, he said, "We're going to catch 'em today. I have been doing this for a while. Let me know if you need some help."

"I'll try and keep up," Bill meekly said.

A jovial group of fishermen on vacation started arriving at 7 o'clock, laughing together as they walked out on the dock toward the boat. Dressed in leisure clothing, they all wore visor caps showing various commercial designs about golf courses and football teams.

Climbing aboard the boat one of them shouted, "Let's go get 'em!"

Bill watched the fishermen crowd around the cooler, where the beer was on ice, wondering if they would be sober enough to fish.

Captain Willis started two big noisy engines while Stan untied the dock lines. The experienced captain swung the 42-foot party boat around, through the inlet and headed for the Gulf Stream.

Stan commenced rigging fishing lines for the fishermen who had no equipment. When Stan noticed Bill standing idle with his group on the port side, he walked over to him and said, "This is what you need to do. Watch me." He picked up one of the rods on the port side and rigged it for one of the fishermen who had no equipment. "Some men have never been on a party-boat. You'll have to rig rods with fishing lines for them."

Bill was a fast learner. He watched Stan rig one of the fishing rods. Stan returned to the starboard side and continued doing the same for inexperienced fishermen on his side of the boat.

Bill saw one of the anglers curiously inspecting one of the rods and said, "Let me show you how to rig it." Bill rigged it the way Stan had just showed him. He handed it to the fishermen and said, "There, you're all ready to catch fish."

By the time the boat reached deepwater, the fishermen were standing around the side, fishing rods in hand, ready to fish. Captain Willis shut down the engines, dropped the anchor and they drifted to a stop over the reef.

"Okay!" somebody yelled, and ten baited lines splashed into the water.

In no time someone on the starboard side shouted, "I got one!"

Bill watched Stan gaff a fifteen-pound grouper and dump it in the fish box at the stern. Bill was ready and the next angler on his side of the boat who hollered, he was at his side with the gaff. Soon fishermen on both sides of the boat were yelling as they pulled on bent rods, and reeled taught lines. Stan and Bill raced back and forth gaffing fish, throwing them into the stern fish box, and baiting lines.

At noon, Captain Willis climbed down from the bridge to the galley and got lunch ready. He set trays of various sandwich meats, taken out of the boat's small refrigerator. At each end of a long table in the galley he opened loaves if sliced bread and plates of sliced tomatoes and lettuce. He put out in the middle of the table mayonnaise, mustard and opened jars of pickles. A basket on the table was filled with packages of potato chips. Under the table, a cooler was stocked with bottles of beer and coke on ice..

Captain Willis went up on deck and yelled, "Come and get lunch."

Bill was pleasantly surprised. He hadn't expected the food but he quickly realized, as part of the crew on board, he and Stan were to be host.

"Here," Bill yelled to one of the anglers bent over the cooler. "I've got the Opener." He joined in with the group crowded around the coke and beer and became popular as he began opening bottles.

At first, Bill didn't know if he should eat too. When he could resist no longer, he joined with the fishermen making their sandwiches, and they all sat around talking about the big one that got away.

By three o'clock, the boxes at the stern were filled with fish. Happy fishermen were drinking one more beer while the boat motored on the way back to the dock. Stan and Bill walked around among them and helped them take down and put away their fishing tackle.

"Another successful day fishing," Captain Willis boasted as he steered the boat back to the dock.

The captain nudged the boat up to the dock. Stan in the bow, and Bill at the stern jumped onto the dock and made the boat lines fast. Bill was sweaty and tired but felt like he was already an experienced deck hand.

Taking fish out of the stern storage boxes and throwing them up on the dock was a job that Bill was asked to do. As the fish piled up on the dock, he felt good about their success catching fish. Stan cleaned fish at a wooden cleaning table and water faucet at the end of the dock. Captain Willis made his way to the pile of fish on the dock as the fishermen were climbing off the boat. He helped them select fish from the pile and received their praise for a good trip. Bill joined Stan at the wooden table cleaning fish. As the fishermen left, they passed by Stan and Bill and took a moment to stuff a five-dollar tip in Stan or Bill's back pocket.

When the last fisherman had driven off, Captain Willis approached the two boys still cleaning fish and said, "That's enough filets. Take them along with the rest of the fish on the dock and put them in back of my truck. I'll sell them at the fish market."

Bill was happy when the captain told him he had done a good job and handed him $10. Pay and tips Bill received was nearly $35 dollars! But he was disappointed when the captain told him the other deck hand was coming back in the morning. His pockets full of cash, he had gained confidence in himself. Canada here I come, he said.

Chapter Eight

THE CIRCUS

It was early and Bill was feeling good standing next to the road with his pack behind him waving his thumb in the air. It felt good last night in the motel as he rolled over in bed and felt the lump of cash in his money belt. He was sorry he had worked only one day on the fishing boat for Captain Willis.

Another day on the road. The highway was beginning to get busy. He was surprised when a pickup truck with four cheering teenagers stopped.

"Jump in the back," one of them yelled. "We're going to the circus."

Crowding into the back of the truck, Bill sat on his pack. It was a wild ride. The teens were having a good time. More than once Bill thought about asking to let him out as they skidded dangerously around curves.

It didn't seem right, Bill was thinking. So many others their age were joining the military to fight for their country. Well, their turn will come, he mused, and they'll be drafted.

They were just getting into the outskirts of Philadelphia when one of the teenagers yelled, " There's the circus! Look at those big tents."

They found a parking place in the lot across the street from the circus and the teenagers jumped out of the truck and headed for the entrance. They were so excited they left Bill standing alone in the parking lot wondering what he was going to do.

"Hey, you," a man standing next to one of the tents shouted at Bill. "You wanna get in free?"

Looking around him, Bill was not sure the man was talking to him. "What do you want?" Bill called back, still not sure.

The big man beckoned to Bill, "I'm looking for someone like you. Come over here and I'll show you how to earn a ticket to get into the show."

Curious, Bill picked up his pack and walked over to the tent and listened to the man explain, "I need you to water our animals. Next to the pump over there is a bucket. Fill it up with water and carry it to the animals inside this tent. Pour it into the troughs at each cage. It's not hard work," he said.

"Okay, I can do that," Bill said.

Bill stashed his pack in the corner of the tent. Feeling lucky to find a way to get tickets into the circus, he picked up a bucket, pumped it full of water, and carried it inside the tent. It was a large tent filled with animals. Caged in big four-wheeled cages, on one side of the tent, tigers paced back and forth.. Separated by a canvas curtain, on the other side of the tent, horses were harnessed. Even though out of sight of the big cats, the horses were nervously straining in their halters with excitement.

Bill found a trough attached to each cage. It could be filled with water from the outside and be in reach of the animals inside the cage.

The man had followed Bill inside the tent where he cautioned, "You must be careful not to reach inside the cages as you water the animals. Once when we were putting on a show in Tucson, we had a Mexican boy who filled the troughs with water. One day he reached inside a cage to pet a tiger and it grabbed his arm and tore it off."

Bill stepped back. The thought of having his arm torn off was shocking.

"If you finish supplying water to the caged animals," the man continued, "give some hay to the horses. But do not feed the animals in their cages," the man grimly warned a second time.

"I'll be very careful," Bill replied earnestly, thinking about a tiger tearing off an arm.

He picked up the bucket and filled it with water. The big man watched Bill perform the water routine for a few moments and left.

It was an exhausting task. Bill saw the tigers watching him as he passed by their cages to the pump. He was careful not to get close.

Bill felt like he was finally catching up with watering, when two trainers burst into the tent and began connecting the harnessed horses to the four-wheeled cages of tigers. As they were pulled outside, Bill followed, wondering what was happening,

A line up was being organized for a parade into the largest circus tent.

The show was about to begin!

From behind a tent flap, where Bill had hidden his pack, he watched a high-sided wagon decorated with painted glass and mirrors, pulled by six prancing horses, lead the parade into the circus tent. Inside the wagon, a calliope loudly tooted a tone that produced stirring marching music. Clowns danced, jumped, somersaulted and waved at the crowd, who were seated in bleachers around the tent. Eight elephants, guided by brightly costumed mahatmas, perched on their necks, lumbered into the circus tent in the parade. Strapped on the backs of the elephants, on bright red sparkling blankets, were sumptuous, canvas-sheltered seats with fluttering blue streamers. Inside each, beautiful girls dressed in brief silver costumes, waved merrily to the crowd. Marching behind them in the parade six golden chariots guided by men in Roman attire were pulled by mustang horses capped with long ostrich feathers waving in the air. Sparkling, caged wagons, pulled by high stepping horses, with pacing tigers inside, added their roars to the resounding music of the calliope. Lion tamers wearing jodhpur breeches, dressage riding boots, safari jackets and western Stetson hats, strutted beside the caged wagons popping whips. Bringing up the end of the parade, a fire engine driven by clowns with long ladders hanging off the back, and ten more clowns prancing around it, as it rolled around inside the big tent.

It was an amazing sight Bill watched as he peeked out at the parade passing by close to his hiding place behind the tent flap. He didn't need a ticket. He had a front row seat.

Bill watched as the wagons were pulled around the track, and then each into one of the three center rings, where they commenced their acts. It was a wild attraction with many acts going on at the same time. The crowd yelled loudly from their bleacher seats.

In one area, tigers were driven from their caged wagons into an enclosed ring. A lion-tamer entered the ring and commanded tigers and lions through their acts.

In another ring, Bill saw trapeze performers demonstrate their daring on high wire apparatus, in the upper areas of the tent. They skillfully swung back and forth, twisting and turning, hand-over-hand exchanging positions on wires suspended from the top of the tent.

Bill watched, in a third ring, clowns who were wearing green shirts, that blossomed around the upper part of their body, were stuffed into red pantaloons held together with big yellow buttons, and purple stockings. In oversized black shoes, with a blue dunce cap, they danced and tumbled around the ring to amuse the crowd.

It was a fantastic view from his unique location at the performer's entrance to the tent. But when the show ended, Bill was beginning to

wonder about strange feelings. This was kid stuff.
He shouldered his pack and left for the highway.
He had more important things to do.

He was going to Canada to join up..

Chapter Nine

THE DELAWARE RIVER
WATER GAP

The highway was crowded with cars leaving the circus. Bill could still hear the circus calliope in the distance. A number of cars passed him as he waved his thumb in the air. A car finally came to a stop just ahead of him on the side of the road.

A young man driving the car dressed in camping clothes said, "Hop in; how far you going?"

Before Bill could answer, the driver said, "I'm headed for the Delaware River Water_Gap to begin a hike into the mountains. It will be late when I get there, but you're welcome to ride along with me as far as I go."

"Well, I'm going in that direction," Bill said. "I'm going to Canada to join the Royal Canadian Air Force."

"Golly, that's great," he said in wonderment. "I'll take you as far as the Gap, near where I plan to camp tonight. You might want to camp there too. There is a highway across the river that I think will take you into Canada."

"Thank you for the ride. I really appreciate it," Bill said.

"My name is Glen Wilson; call me Glen. We'll be traveling along the Delaware River. It's a scenic route that I enjoy traveling. I believe you will enjoy seeing it before it gets too dark. I'd like to hear about your trip to join the Royal Canadian Air Force"

"I'll write you a book about it," Bill said jokingly. It's a trip I'm looking forward to, but for now you'll have to tell me about camping in the water gap."

"It's an unspoiled area next to about 200,000 acres owned by the state of New Jersey for a wilderness reservation. I really like it there," Glen said.

When they arrived, it was late but still light enough to see the river flowing through the gap in the mountains that forms the Delaware River Water Gap.

"What a view," Bill said. "All the water of this broad river has cut its way through the mountains over the years."

"It's a powerful force," Glen commented. "See how the river rushes through in rapids as it plows its way past big boulders."

"What an amazing sight," Bill said, "even in the dim light of the evening."

Glen parked the car a short distance past the Gap in an open area where a small creek tumbled out of the mountains into the river. "This is a remote place where it's great to camp," Glen said. "From here it's an overnight hike back into the interior where few people go."

"Why would you want to hike back in those mountains?" Bill asked.

"The Appalachian Trail passes along the ridges of these mountains. I'm meeting two of my friends at a checkpoint on the trail that overlooks the Gap. I'm looking forward to hiking with them a short distance. There are many rare plants and many kinds of wild animals along The Appalachian Trail as it winds through undisturbed wilderness. It's not unusual to see deer, bear, and someone reported seeing a mountain lion. Why don't you come along and join us? I'll only be hiking with them a few miles into New York

State, where another friend will be giving me a ride back here in his car."

"No. Thank you," Bill said. "It's in the right direction, but I don't have time for hiking. I've got to be going on my trip to Canada."

"I'm going to camp here and start hiking in the morning," Glen said. "Maybe you'd like to camp here too. There are not many cars that pass here this late. You'll have a better chance of catching a ride in the morning on the highway across the river. There's an old abandoned railroad trestle nearby that I think you can cross over to the highway."

"That sounds great," Bill said. "I'd like the company."

Looking around him, as the stream gurgled by into the Delaware River, Bill said, "This stream looks like it might have some trout. I'll bet I can catch enough for dinner before it gets dark."

"Okay," Glen said, "you supply the fish and I have a can of beans to go along with them."

It didn't take Bill long to cut down a long straight sapling, just the right size for a fishing pole. Out of his pack, he took out a coil of line with a fishhook attached and tied it to the end of the pole. Under rocks near the stream in damp soil, he found insect larva for bait. Bill quietly sneaked up to a promising pool in the stream, cast in the baited hook and immediately pulled out the first trout. It was still flopping on the shore when he pulled a second trout out of the same pool. He quit when he had six trout.

Glen already had a fire going with some bacon crackling in a frying pan. Bill cleaned the fish, cutting them into filets, which sizzled as he laid them in the frying pan with the hot bacon grease. In the meantime, Glen had put an open can of beans in the hot coals at the edge of the campfire.

Together with fried filets and heated beans, Glen and Bill made a meal on tin plates from Glen's pack.

"It would be nice," Glen said with a smile, "if you could supply some cold cans of beer from your pack."

"I can't, but how about some cold water?" Bill joked.

After dinner, they unrolled their sleeping bags near the campfire and as the night closed in around them, Bill was ready for sleep. The sky was clear and bright stars lit up the heaven.

Across the river, he saw automobile lights moving back and forth on a busy highway.

"You should be able to get a ride over there tomorrow," Glen commented.

"If I can get across the river on that old railroad trestle," Bill sleepily said. "If I just can ...," and he was asleep.

The dark sky was just beginning to light up on the eastern horizon the next morning when Bill and Glen rolled out of their sleeping bags and started to break camp.

Bill stoked up the campfire with fresh wood on last night's coals.

"I'll fix a light breakfast," Bill said. "You save your supplies. Where you're going, there's no place to buy food."

While Glen was cinching up his backpack, Bill put a pot of water on the fire. He poured some oatmeal into the pot of boiling water. He sweetened the thickened hot oatmeal with a liberal amount of sugar from his pack. As it was cooling warm enough to eat, he also fixed two cups of boiling water with some instant coffee.

"Some day, I hope we can get together again," Glen joked. "You make a pretty good cook." Then more seriously he said, "The way the war is going, who knows, we might be meeting in the military some place overseas."

"After the war is over," Bill said, "I hope we will both be able to come back so we can again, share a campfire up in these woods. I'd like to make that hike with you to the Appalachian Trail."

They sat back in silence around the fire as they savored the food. Their uncertainties about the war caused a heavy silence.

Suddenly, Glen said, "The car will be safe parked here while I'm gone. Now, I gotta go! Maybe we can someday meet on a battlefield." He shouldered his pack, said goodbye, and hiked off up the stream, into the mountains, toward the Appalachian Trail.

Chapter Ten

FRIGHTENING MOMENTS

The dawn was breaking with a clear blue sky by the time Bill cleaned up the campsite. He lifted his backpack onto his shoulders and headed off down the old road toward the railroad trestle.

Bill could see the old railroad bed where it ran on top of the high riverbank. The rails that once ran across the river had been taken away when metal was being salvaged for the war. But the trestle was still standing with long, rusty I-beams stretching across the river from concrete stanchion to concrete stanchion. It was a way across.

He climbed onto the tracks where they stretched out from the top of bank over the river.

At first Bill walked upright, balanced on a narrow I-beam. The bank underneath sloped away beneath him, as he walked across on the beam. Bill could see the ground under him get further and further away. When he was over the river, standing on the I-beam, the water was several hundred feet below. The distance, as he looked down, was frightening.

The wind began to blow.

Bill felt the wind blowing against him and his pack in gusts. It seemed like the trestle was swaying and he had trouble maintaining his balance. He sat down astraddle the beam, terrified, and watched pieces of rust, he had dislodged, fall down, down through space and splash into the river far below. It took a few moments before he stopped shaking and began to scoot along the beam where he was sitting, pulling himself forward slowly, inch by inch.

Sweating and covered with rust from the old iron I-beams, Bill made it across to the top of the riverbank on the other side. He rolled off the beam onto the ground and laid there panting as he stopped shaking and recovered from his fright.

This side of the river was in Pennsylvania. He looked around and saw he was now in a deserted woodland area beside the remains of the old railroad trestle. Through the trees, a busy highway was visible not far away.

Down the embankment, the Delaware River flowed through the mountain gap. Bill decided to clean himself of the rust on his body and clothes. He slid down the embankment, took off his pack, undressed, and gingerly waded through the river shallows until he was swimming in deep water. The cool water felt good. He enjoyed a leisurely swim in the solitude of this remote area for a longer time than he had planned.

He came ashore and inspected the rust-covered clothes on the ground where he had undressd. A thorough rinsing in the river and he managed to remove most of the rust and dirt accumulated on his clothing. Wringing them out as best as he could, Bill hung them on a bush to dry. He tried to ignore a festered blister on his left hand that began to itch as he dressed in a spare set of clothes from his pack. Exhausted, he laid down in the shade of a tree and went to sleep.

The shrill scream of an osprey overhead awoke him where he rested near the trestle. He watched for a moment as the osprey swooped down over the water and grasped a fish in its talons.

The day was half gone as Bill stretched were he stood up on the bank, feeling revived.

His clothes hanging in the sun on the bush were still damp but dry enough, he decided, to fold up into his pack.

Shouldering his backpack, Bill hiked to the nearby busy road. His hand itched and he rubbed it against his pants.

Traffic was heavy, going both ways on the highway. Bill lifted his thumb, signaling for a ride going north. A maroon Dodge sedan slowed down and pulled off on the side of the road. The driver, a young man, leaned out the window and said, "I'm going to Scranton."

"That's good," Bill said. "I'm going in that direction. Scranton is on my way to Canada."

"Hop in," the driver said.

As Bill put his backpack in the back and climbed into the front seat, he said, "I'm going to Canada to join the Royal Canadian Air Force."

"Wow!" The driver said. "I've heard a lot about the R.C.A.F. I'm going to join the Marines when I get out of college. My name is Ralph. I'm in my senior year at the University of Pennsylvania."

"Some day, when the war is over, I'm going to go to the University of Florida," Bill said.

"Hey, you'll be a Gator. We play football with them every year. They usually have a good team. We beat them this year, but last year we lost."

The ride was a long discussion about football. When they reached Scranton, Bill thanked Ralph for the ride as he got out of the car in the outskirts of the city on the highway going to Canada. Bill watched as Ralph drove off in another direction. His hand was beginning to ache as he turned to face traffic with his thumb in the air.

Chapter Eleven

THE OLD MAN

A number of cars passed as he thumbed for a ride. Finally, an old model A Ford creeping along the highway came to a stop. Cars following behind had to suddenly slow down and maneuver around the Ford that was still halfway on the road. Bill walked up to the car, looking in the open side window. He saw the driver was an old man. Almost bald and with a smile showing missing teeth, he leaned over the seat and shouted over the noise of his engin, "Get in quick before we get run over."

Bill opened the car door and slid in holding his pack on his lap. Before he said anything the man said, "How far you going?"

Looking critically at the old instrument panel and cracked windshield, Bill wondered how far they would be going before the car broke down. He said, "I'm headed for Canada."

"That's a long way," the man said as he shifted the car up to speed into the traffic he had slowed down. "I'm only going as far as Binghamton. It's just across the state line into New York."

Looking at the condition of the old car, Bill was hoping they made it that far and said, "I appreciate the ride. I've been unable to get one. Most everybody is in a hurry to go somewhere."

"Yeah," the man said, "the highway is really crowded. Everybody seems like they're in a hurry these days. I ain't in a hurry."

While they talked, the old Ford was laboring to climb the steep roads in the Catskill Mountains. All at once, the car lurched and there was a loud popping noise as the engine stopped.

"Uh oh," the man said as he steered the car, coasting to a stop off the edge of the road. He opened the door, climbed out, walked around to the front of the car, opened the hood, and looked inside at the engine.

Bill, still in the front seat with his pack on his lap, heard the man exclaim, "My god!" He walked around to Bill's side of the car and said through the window, "You ought to see the engine. You ain't gonna believe it." He put his hands together, formed a circle and said, "There's a hole in the engine block this big!"

Bill shook his head in amazement. This was the end of this ride.

Just then, a pickup truck pulled off the road behind them and a man leaned out his window and shouted, "Hey, Jerry. What's the matter? You having trouble?"

"It's my friend, Sam," Jerry said to Bill. Then he shouted back to Sam, "My engine's shot. Can you give me a push? There's a garage I know of a short distance down the road."

Sam pulled up behind them in his pickup and pushed them back onto the road, down the highway.

Bill was still sitting in the car, holding his pack in his lap, nervously wondering what Jerry was going to do.

Jerry honked his horn as he steered back into traffic, signaling out his window to Sam with his hand to keep pushing.

Three agonizing miles down the highway, Bill was stressfully pushing his feet on the floorboards of the car. Jerry signaled to Sam, pushing behind, that he was making a turn and then waved him off as he coasted off the road into the parking lot in front of a garage. A sign on the front of the building read, "We repair cars."

Bill was recovering from his agonizing ride, as Jerry walked into the garage and told a mechanic, "I'm having car trouble."

Leading the mechanic behind him, Jerry walked back out to his car and said to him, "How long will it take to fix my car?"

It took only a second after looking at the engine for the mechanic to say, "This old car is finished. There's no way I can fix a hole like that in the engine block. To replace that engine, if I could find one that old, would cost more than this car is worth."

"Well, how much will you give me for the car?" Jerry said.

"For the scrap and spare parts, it's only worth about $50," was the reply.

Bill was climbing out of the old car with his pack when he heard Jerry say, "Okay, I'll take it."

Jerry waved at Sam, who was idling his pickup truck, waiting out front of the garage, and shouted, "Wait a minute for us. We're going to need a ride. I'm selling my old car."

Counting the money as he walked back outside the garage, Jerry said to Bill, who was still standing outside next to the old car holding his pack, "Come on. Climb in the back of the pickup with Sam. My friend will give us a ride to my house."

Bill didn't know what to say. It was a ride, he thought. He threw his pack in back of the pickup and climbed in.

Jerry opened the front door of the pickup on the passenger side, stepped in with Sam and they all drove off, down the highway.

Hanging onto his pack as he bounced along in the rear of the pickup, Bill was wondering where they were going. Beside, his hand was still hurting. Well, he decided, they were going in the right direction, toward Canada.

It was a long drive through traffic and it was getting late.

Then he saw the sign:

CITY LIMITS
BINGHAMTON, N.Y.
Population: 42,845

Bill rapped on the rear window of the pickup truck where he saw Sam driving and Jerry in the passenger seat. Jerry slid open the window.

"Where are we going?" Bill shouted over the engine noise of the truck.

"We're going to my house," Jerry replied. "It's getting late. You can stay at my house. I have a couch that unfolds into a bed."

Better than sleeping on the ground somewhere in the woods, Bill was thinking.

They arrived at a four-room shack that Jerry called home on the outskirts of Binghamton. "This is my home," Jerry explained to Bill. "It has everything I need and where I can be independent of my children. In addition to the bedroom, there is a couch in the living room, that unfolds into a bed. You can be comfortable here until you go on your way to Canada tomorrow."

Jerry turned to Sam, still waiting in his truck and said, "Thanks for the ride. I'll be okay until I buy another car when my Social Security check comes in next month. In the meantime, there is a good bus line here, I can get around on."

Sam drove off with a wave of his hand and Jerry said to Bill, "Come on, I'll show you around."

While he was conducting a tour of the house there was a knock on the front door.

"Hey Helen," Jerry said. "Come in."

"I saw you come home," Helen said to Jerry. "How was your drive to Philadelphia? Did you have a good visit with your daughter?"

An elderly woman about the same age as Jerry, dressed in her house smock, stepped into the house.

Jerry called out to Bill standing in the living room, "Meet Helen. She's a neighbor from across the street, and a good friend."

"Yeah," Helen said, "we've known each other long enough so that every time Jerry runs out of sugar he knocks on my door." She turned to Jerry and said, "I brought you some meatloaf I just made. I thought you would be hungry after your long trip," She handed Jerry a shopping bag. "There's some fresh tomatoes in the bag, too, from my garden. I think there's enough for both of you."

"Thank you. I was just getting ready to fix dinner .... " Jerry started to say when he was suddenly interrupted.

"Where is your car?" Helen asked.

"That old car finally broke down and I sold it," Jerry said. "I'm gonna have to see if I can buy another one that's in better shape. In the meantime I'll have to use the bus to do my shopping."

"I'm going shopping at the store in the morning," Helen said. "I'll be glad to give you a ride."

"Hey, that's great. I need to get some groceries." Jerry said. "Also, Bill needs to get back on his way in the morning. Maybe you can give him a ride to the highway where he can hitch a ride to Canada. He's going to join the Royal Canadian Air Force."

"Sure. I'll be happy to give him a ride. He looks like someone the Canadians can use to fight those awful Germans," Helen said with a smile.

Bill replied with a grin, "Thank you. It's nice of you to offer. When I get overseas I'll shoot a German just for you."

They both laughed.

"Okay, I'll pick you both up at about 9 o'clock tomorrow morning," Helen said as she went out the door.

After she left, Jerry said to Bill, "Now you make yourself at home while I fix us something to eat from what Helen brought."

They enjoyed dinner together and sat around the table for hours talking about their lives.

Bill was the first to yawn. He apologized and said, "Its been a long day." As he got up to leave the table, he winced when he bumped his hand on the edge of the table.

Rubbing his hand, Bill said, "My hand is really sore."

"I've got some petroleum jelly you can rub on. It helps me a lot with my aches and pains," Jerry said as he got up from the table to get the medicine.

That night, Bill snuggled down in the bed made up from the couch. He thought the ointment gave him some relief from his sore hand.

In the morning, Jerry was up early and had a breakfast of bacon and eggs prepared by the time Bill was packed and ready to go.

"How's your hand?" Jerry inquired.

"It's still sore and swollen this morning," Bill replied, "but I think it will feel better after I'm up and around."

Promptly at 9 o'clock, Helen was out front in her car, honking the horn.

It was a short ride to the highway. Too little time, Bill felt afterward, for him to say thank you. Bill stepped out of the car on the road and Jerry and Helen waved good-bye as they drove off to the shopping mall.

Another place, and two more people he would remember after the war, Bill thought as he walked up to the edge of the highway with his thumb in the air.

Chapter Twelve

BLOOD POISON!

A dozen cars passed before a late model Buick pulled off the road and stopped ahead of the hitchhiker.

"Hot dog, a ride already," Bill said aloud to himself as he grabbed up his pack, and ran to the car.

"Get in," a well-dressed gentleman said through the side window.

Bill opened the back door, put his pack onto the back seat, and climbed into the front. As he had been loading the pack with his left hand, Bill cried out in pain.

Back into traffic, the driver settled the car down to a comfortable speed and broke the silence, "How far you going?" he said.

Bill hesitated to answer. Impressed by the courteous air of the driver, he decided to tell the truth. "I'm going to Ottawa, Canada."

With a smile, the driver glanced at Bill saying, "I'm coming from a medical convention in Scranton, going home to Syracuse. It's about 150 miles. I can take you that far."

"You a doctor?" Bill asked. He had a lot of respect for doctors.

"Yes, I am," the driver replied.

There was silence as miles ticked away. Bill was beginning to feel queasy and feverish from his infected hand. Trying to get up the nerve to say something he said, "My hand has been hurting. I'm worried about it. Would you look at it?"

Looking over at Bill, the doctor asked, "How did you hurt your hand?"

Embarrassed by the attention, but hurting too much to refuse help from the doctor, Bill said, "A blister on my hand got infected and it's swollen and hurts."

At a wide place in the road, the doctor pulled off and stopped the car. He turned in his seat and said, "Let me see your hand." He looked at the swollen fingers on Bill's left hand and then asked him to roll up his sleeve. He studied the red streaks going up the arm then turned back in his seat, started the car, and drove back into traffic on the highway.

After a few minutes, the doctor said, "That's a serious infection that needs medical attention. Tell me," he curiously said, "where are you really going?"

Wincing as he rolled his sleeve back down, but without hesitation, Bill rushed his reply. "I'm going to Canada to join the Royal Canadian Air Force."

The doctor smiled and then became serious. "You'll never make it with that hand. That's a bad case of blood poisoning. If you don't get attention soon, the hand and maybe the whole arm will have to be amputated."

Cut off his hand! Cut off his arm! It was only an infected hand, Bill solemnly thought.

The doctor continued, "I think I should take you to the hospital where you can get that hand taken care of."

Maybe he should do what the doctor said, Bill thought.

"Okay, if it won't take too long," he said.

It seemed like a long drive before they arrived at a two-story brick building, spread over a block with lots of windows. On front was a sign with two-foot high letters, "SYRACUSE GENERAL HOSPITAL."

The doctor drove around to the side of the building marked "EMERGENCY" and Bill stepped out, pulling his pack out onto the ground beside the car. The doctor rolled down his window and said, "Go inside and ask for Dr. Perry. He's the resident physician. Tell him you have blood poison from an infection on your hand and that Dr. Mathews sent you. I'll check in on you later."

The doctor drove away leaving Bill standing on the sidewalk with his pack at his side looking at the entrance with anxiety. He had better go inside, he thought.

Groaning with pain from his swollen hand and arm, Bill picked up his pack with his good hand and started for the door.

Inside, the nurse on duty looked at him standing in the lobby. "Can I help you?" she said in a pleasant voice.

"Dr. Mathews told me I should ask Dr. Perry to look at my hand. He said I have blood poisoning. My hand and arm is swollen and it's worrying me. Maybe I can get some medicine to cure it so I can be on my way."

The nurse looked at the hand and the arm extending from Bill's shirt. His wrist and knuckles were no longer visible in the swollen flesh. "Wait here," she said, "I'll get Dr. Perry."

Boy, this is some place, Bill observed as he anxiously waited. He was beginning to wonder how long he was going to have to stay. I hope they can get me out of here so I can make camp today before it gets too dark, he said to himself.

A short, fat, middle-aged man in a white jacket with a stethoscope draped around his neck came into the lobby with the nurse.

He walked up to Bill and said, "I'm Dr. Perry. Let me see your hand."

After examining his hand, the doctor pulled up the sleeve of Bill's shirt and looked at the arm. He reached inside the shirt and felt the armpit. When he pressed a lump discovered under the arm, Bill flinched.

"Ow!" he said. "That hurt."

The doctor turned his back to Bill and quietly said to the nurse, "We'll have to amputate if we can't stop the infection from spreading. Put the arm and hand in an ice vat and let's try that new antibiotic, penicillin. I hear it's working well with the wounded in the war."

Bill heard him! This wasn't something for which they were going to give him a little medicine and send him on his way.

Looking at Bill's frightened expression the nurse calmly said, "Come with me. We're going to put you in bed and take care of that infection."

Bed! She said bed, Bill was thinking. This was more serious than he thought.

On the second floor, the nurse led Bill into a ward, where he saw six other beds, each cloaked privately behind white screens. She handed Bill a folded blue hospital gown saying, "The floor nurse will be with you soon and explain everything to you." She turned and walked out of the ward.

A pretty nurse with a white cap on her blond hair came into the ward, dressed in white clothes that rustled as she walked.

"Hi! My name is Ruth. I understand you have an infected hand. I'll bet it hurts." Without waiting for a reply she continued, "Don't worry, we'll take good care of you. Bring your gown and come with me. I'll show you where the shower is."

While he showered he was unable to use his infected hand and the ache in his arm made him feel ill. Bill struggled, using one hand, into the hospital gown. Back in the ward, he noticed that his old clothes were gone. Nurse Ruth pulled down the sheets, patted the mattress and said, "Do you need some help getting into bed?"

Holding his sore left arm stiffly aside, Bill pulled himself onto the bed, trying not to expose himself from the loose-fitting gown in front of a pretty nurse. The hand was beginning to hurt more and he felt dizzy after his climb into bed.

Ruth tucked in the sheets and said, "What's your name?"

Ruth was a good looking woman, with a smile that took away his breath. She seemed so considerate as she fluffed his pillow. Why not tell her the truth, he thought.

"My name is Bill. I'm on the way to Canada to join the Royal Canadian Air Force."

"Where are you from, and what is your parents' name?" she asked.

Bill looked the other way and didn't say any thing. He wasn't ready for his parents to know his situation which he was beginning to think was more serious than he thought. Before they were told anything, he wanted to be out of here and in the Air Force.

After a moment Ruth said, "Don't worry, you don't have to tell me. I won't ask any more questions. I'm here to make you well. Take this medication. It will take away some of the pain and help you relax." She held out in her hand two pills and a glass of water in the other hand.

Bill swallowed the pills with a gulp of water without hesitation. He looked at Ruth and asked, "How long will it take to make me well?"

"Not long. Now you rest. I'll be back to look in on you in a little while."

When the nurse left, Bill began to look around his surroundings. He could hear someone coughing beyond the screen around his bed. Someone else was moaning. Not far away he heard whispering voices from another direction. He was not alone. Others shared this room with the high ceiling and rows of indirect lighting. He looked at his swollen hand and arm. What was going to happen to him?

Home was a long way away. Mother would have hovered over his bed, felt his forehead with a tender hand, and taken his temperature. Dad would come home from work and he would hear him downstairs asking Mother about him. What are they doing now, Bill wondered as his eyelids became heavy and he fell into a deep sleep.

Chapter Thirteen

END OF THE JOURNEY

He was cold. Bill struggled to wake. His senses slowly intensified as he felt the chill in his arm. When he opened his eyes, he saw a long tub next to him where he lay in bed on his back in the hospital. The tub was filled with ice water and there was an arm submerged in it. He came fully awake and realized he was connected to the arm in the tub of ice water.

Standing next to the bed, he saw Ruth as she smiled reassuringly as she gently held his arm under the ice water. It was cold but his arm didn't hurt as bad, as it had.

A small incision was made at the location of the infection to assist draining. Two days of shots, pills and chills passed before Bill noticed the swelling in his hand was going down. Ruth, who had become special to Bill with her constant care and compassion, explained the infection in his arm was draining. "Your hand will be healed as good as new. You came close to losing your arm," she told him.

"I appreciate all you've done. You've been so good to me." Then he looked down at his arm and said, "When will I be able to leave?"

He was beginning to think again about his trip to Canada to join-up.

Bill was surprised to hear Ruth say, "The hospital will want to discharge you in the next few days, and they will need to know who will be continuing with the medical care of your hand."

Bill bowed his head and, disappointed, said, "I didn't know my treatment would have to continue."

Ruth said, "You will need to have a doctor frequently change the packing in the cavity left by the infection. After the infected area has healed, and the packing is removed, the wound will have to be stitched while it is healing. You need to go home where your doctor can take care of you."

Laying back on his pillow he sadly said, "It's been so long since I left home."

"We can call your parents on the telephone," Ruth said. "I'm sure they will be glad to hear from you and know you are all right."

"I don't know what to say," Bill murmured.

Ruth smiled and said, "You can explain you're in the hospital with a serious infection in your hand. I'm sure they will be glad to hear from you."

He had missed home and near tears Bill said, "Do you think they will want to come get me?"

"I'm sure of it," she said.

Ruth had always been so kind and capable in his treatment, Bill was thinking. It was hard for him to ignore her suggestion.

"Okay," he responded to Ruth, "I'll call home and tell them what has happened."

Bill's mother answered the telephone when he called. She immediately knew who it was, and said, "Bill! Bill, how are you? Where are you?"

It was so good to hear her voice. At first, it was difficult for him to talk.

"Mom … Mom," he stammered. "I'm in the hospital in Syracuse, New York, and I have an infected hand." Gathering strength, he said, "The doctor says I'm all right now, but that I need to have a doctor continue with my treatment when I leave the hospital. I want to come home."

"Of course," she almost shouted in relief. "Your father and I have been so worried about you."

Nurse Ruth tapped Bill on the shoulder, who was having difficulty talking and said, "Let me talk to your mother."

"Hello, I am Bill's nurse," she said, "He had a serious infection in his hand. You don't have to worry, we've been able to treat the infection. Bill will be ready for discharge from the hospital in the next few days."

Ruth held the telephone up close to Bill and said, "You talk."

Near tears he said, "I've missed you so much, Mom."

"Your father and I love you very much," she said. "Dad will come to Syracuse and pick you up right away."

After she hung up, Ruth turned to Bill, smiled, and said, "Your mother sounds very nice."

Bill shifted his head against the pillow and didn't know what to say. He was crying.

The next day, Bill awoke to the presence of someone new standing beside his bed. He looked up to see a tall, slim man, his dark hair combed straight back, and a thin mustache over lips that were smiling. He immediately recognized him.

"Hello, son," the man said.

It was a long moment before Bill recovered from his surprise at his arrival so soon. "Hi, Dad," he managed to say in a weak voice.

They both looked at each other. Dad touched Bill's shoulder gently and broke the silence: "Son, do you want to come home?"

"Yes, Dad," he emotionally replied, very nearly in tears.

*   *   *   *   *   *

They walked down the stairs of the hospital, father and son, to the waiting taxi.

Bill waved to Nurse Ruth standing near the door. She was smiling, but there was a tear in her eye as she waved good-bye.

The driver closed the doors of the taxi, turned and asked his passengers, "Where to?"

"Home," father and son said in unison.